DOES A FIDDLER CRAB FIDDLE?

By Corinne Demas
and Artemis Roehrig

Paintings by John Sandford

PERSNICKETY
PRESS

For Morgan, Devon, Ariadne, and Demetria — cd, ar

For Crab Master Jacques Laramie — js

Text copyright © 2016 by Corinne Demas
and Artemis Roehrig
Paintings copyright © 2016 by John Sandford

Designed by Hans Teensma, Impress

CPSIA Tracking Label Information
Production Location: Guangdong, China
Production Date: 5/1/2016
Cohort: Batch 1

ISBN 978-1943978-03-8
10 9 8 7 6 5 4 3 2 1

Published by Persnickety Press

Does a fiddler crab fiddle?

No!
But his one enormous claw looks like a fiddle.
He waves it so other crabs will think he's tough.

Does a fiddler crab
build a sandcastle?

No!
But he digs a hole a foot deep in the saltmarsh.
He piles balls of sand from his tunnel by his front door.

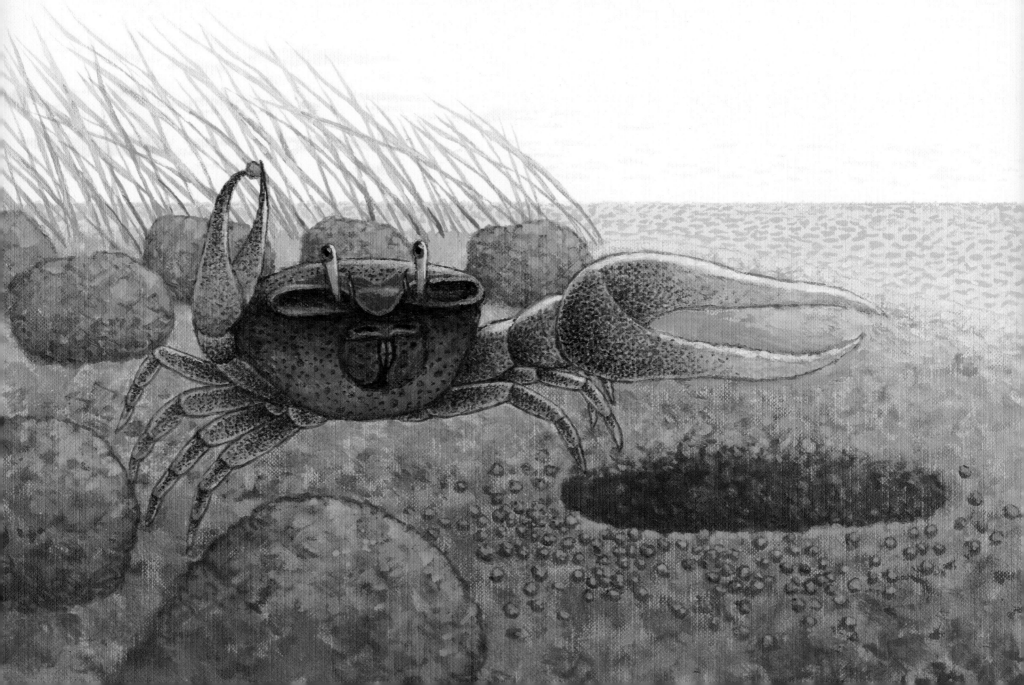

Does a fiddler crab use a snorkel?

No!
But when the tide comes up
he scuttles to his hole and breathes air
that is trapped inside.

No!
But he gobbles up saltmarsh muck, swallows everything yummy, and spits out little pellets of sand.

Does a fiddler crab do magic tricks?

No!
But his shell can change color.
It gets darker or lighter
to help him hide.

Does a fiddler crab wear sunglasses?

No!
But he has eyes on stalks so he
can see all around and look out for danger.

Does a fiddler crab ride a skateboard?

No!
But he runs sideways to the left or the right so the shore birds can't catch him.

Does a fiddler crab listen to the radio?

No!
But he can feel the vibrations
of your footsteps when you
try to creep up close.

Does a fiddler crab use a bandage?

No!
But if he loses one of his two claws,
or one of his eight walking legs . . .

. . . he can grow it back again.

Does a fiddler crab fly south when it gets cold?

No!
All winter long he sleeps safe in his tunnel . . .

. . . until warm spring comes again.

Authors' Note

THERE ARE ninety-seven species of fiddler crabs. Common along the Atlantic seacoast (where the non-fictional pages of this book are set), the sand fiddler crab (*Uca pugilator*) lives in sand, while the mud fiddler crab (*Uca pugnax*) lives in mud.

Fiddler crabs breathe through gills, which they must keep moist. That's why they live close to water. Only the males have a single, enlarged claw (females have two small ones)—sometimes the right, sometimes the left. They use it to attract females and scare off other males. Occasionally males will fight over territory and mates, but it's mostly bluff. They rarely hurt each other.

Fiddler crabs are detritivores, which means that they eat decaying plants and animals. They scoop up sediment with their small front claws. Females scoop with two claws, while the males use just their one small claw. They have specialized mouths which enable them to scrape out the food particles.

Two weeks after mating, females release their eggs into the water. The eggs—several thousand of them—hatch into larvae. It takes a year for them to develop into adult crabs. Adults live a year or two. Like all crustaceans, they molt their exoskeletons to get bigger, since they don't have bones that grow inside them.

Predators of fiddler crabs include fish, raccoons, and birds. One type of shorebird, the Whimbrel, has a specialized beak just the right size for poking into fiddler crabs' holes. Currently the greatest threat to fiddler crabs is humans. Development, especially along the coast of California, has destroyed a lot of fiddler crab habitat.

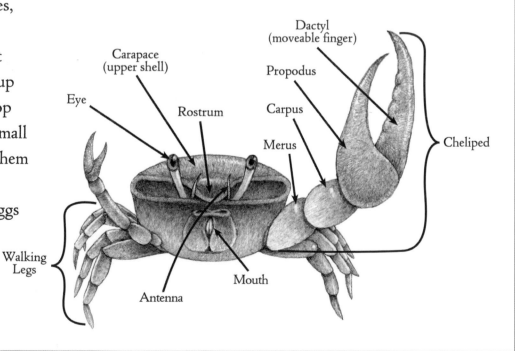